The

Proposing
Tree

Also by James F. Twyman

Emissary of Light: A Vision of Peace

Prayer of St. Francis

Emissary of Love: The Psychic Children Speak to the World

The

Proposing Tree

a love story by

JAMES F. TWYMAN

Author of *Emissary of Love*

HAMPTON ROADS
PUBLISHING COMPANY, INC.

Cover design by Marjoram Productions
Cover illustration © 2003 Anne L. Louque

Hampton Roads Publishing Company, Inc.
1125 Stoney Ridge Road
Charlottesville, VA 22902

434-296-2772
fax: 434-296-5096
e-mail: hrpc@hrpub.com
www.hrpub.com

If you are unable to order this book from your local
bookseller, you may order directly from the publisher.
Call 1-800-766-8009, toll-free.

Library of Congress Cataloging-in-Publication Data

Twyman, James F.
   The proposing tree : a love story / James F. Twyman.
      p. cm.
   ISBN 1-57174-394-4 (acid-free paper)
   1. Santa Monica (Calif.)--Fiction. I. Title.
   PS3620.W96P76 2003
    813'.54--dc21

                              2003011602

ISBN 1-57174-394-4
10 9 8 7 6 5 4 3 2 1
Printed on acid-free paper in the United States

Dedication

This is the story of a real tree in Los Angeles. Thank you for taking me there, Jennifer, and I hope you remember some of these words, reflections of my soul that you alone heard and loved. I said many of them to you, though it was all just a game we played. Still, our hearts are forever joined, and the seeds we planted beneath that tree continue to grow strong. That is why I am dedicating this book to you.

Our love is timeless, as is this story.

Chapter One

The tree: It is the sort of round, mighty oak that many people only imagine exists, since it is rarely seen by human eyes. Its branches plume like a soft cloud, green and full, and its base is more like three trunks than one, winding and twisting around each other before finally joining together as a single broad life. It would be easy, if one were driving by in a car, to look past it altogether and miss the majestic way it leans out over the street there on the corner of 2nd and Windsor. There are many lovely trees in that Los Angeles neighborhood, but none compare to the Proposing Tree, as it is now called, for there is magic beneath its branches.

The young boy didn't notice any of this, only that the branches were strong and it was an easy climb. His parents bought the house only a few months earlier and he felt like a king every time he rose above the yard, held safe in the arms of his new friend. There was only one compromise he had to make to continue this passion. He could only climb the tree when his mother was present, normally sitting on the nearby front porch reading a book, or staring off into space wondering when it would be her turn to live the adventures she envisioned.

That particular summer day was not much different from any other. The air was sticky and hot, and the boy imagined that climbing even a few feet above the Earth would take him into the cooler atmosphere where he could breathe again. He was a steady climber, occasionally taking a risk or two so it wouldn't get too boring, but always aware that at least one of his mother's eyes was fixed upon him.

He was on his way back down the tree when he saw something stuffed in the "V" where two main branches came together, seven feet from the ground. He leaned forward to see what it was and noticed the sealed plastic container just big enough to contain the distinct hand-stitched binding of a homemade book, much like the one he made in school weeks earlier. He pried it from the grip of the tree and took a closer look.

He opened the plastic and read the title that was printed on the cover: "The Proposing Tree. By Fredrick James." beneath this there was one line that was hard to read having been exposed to natural elements. It said: "This is my gift to you, Great Friend." After thumbing through a page or two the boy realized it wasn't much value to him and called down to his mother.

"Mom, I found a book or something. It looks like someone hid it up here."

The woman set down the novel she was reading and looked up at the boy, shading her eyes from the bright sun. "Bring it down and show it to me," she said to him.

He jumped from the lowest branch to the ground, something the woman always hated to see, and ran over to where she sat. She glanced at the cover and opened it to the first page.

"It's not really a book, more of a notebook," she said to her son. "Look, someone spent a great deal of time writing this out by hand. I wonder what it's all about."

"Why don't you read it and find out?" the boy said as he skipped back to the tree. It was an obvious reply, one that often comes from the mouth of a child, the sort of wisdom adults need to listen to more often.

"Why not," she said beneath her breath. "The other book is boring anyway, and this smells like an adventure. Who knows what I'll learn."

And so she began to read the story of the tree, written by the man who knew it better than anyone else. Why it was *hidden in the branches of the oak was still a mystery, but each word brought her closer to the truth. Within minutes, she was completely engrossed.*

This story is my gift to you, Great Tree. Of all the books I've written this is the most important; though no one else will ever read these words. It is a story you know well, for you witnessed the whole affair and you heard every word that was ever said beneath these branches. There is no place on this Earth, save this very spot I now stand, where my heart has been more open and my mind more clear. You are like a silent clock that has marked my days and remembered every meaningful word I ever said. You deserve to hear the whole story, then, and to know how it all ends.

You are the Proposing Tree. Do you realize that? It's impossible for me to know if you understand what has happened here in your shadow, all the events that have shaped our love these last forty years. I had known Carolyn for six months when we found you, and it's true that I loved her from the first moment we met. Our lives coil around each other, just as your roots wrap themselves around this moist Earth. Even the fragile twigs that stretch furthest from the ground have felt the rapture of this joining. You have beheld our long journey to love and are the judge that heard our words, remembering them for us to one day claim. If I had sufficient words to thank you for your gift I would surely offer them. Hopefully my devotion is enough, both to you and the woman I love. That is the only thing I can offer now. Devotion, after all, is the only thing that really matters in this world.

Has time really moved so fast that I now reflect upon these events as if they were a dream? You are the only thing that has not changed at all, Great Tree, though your arms now claim the sky with greater authority than when I was young. We, on the other hand, have aged and matured, but we have gained a perspective that was impossible when we first met. It's hard to believe that forty years have passed since we noticed you on the corner of 2nd and Windsor. Thank God we stopped to look upon your greatness that day, for you symbolize everything that is important in both our lives.

Where do I begin? I have told so many stories this lifetime, but none of them struck so close to my heart than the one I am about to describe. It feels important to give you a full reckoning, to explain all the things you could not have learned from the conversations we had beneath your branches. Maybe I am doing it more for myself than you, for it helps me examine the life I shared with Carolyn, the opportunity to look beneath the crease of our winding relationship and discover the truth that has eluded us till now. Whatever the reason, it feels good to talk to you again, the way I used to talk to you, and to bare myself in a way I normally cannot.

I had always been a solitary pilgrim wandering through life without ever really committing to it. Had it not been for Carolyn I may have never changed. Writing was my way of waving off any real existence, choosing instead a world that existed in my mind, a world I could change at will depending upon whatever story I was weaving at the time. When I was in high school I discovered I had a talent for writing and I used it to escape from the mundane world my parents had built around us. There were six of us living in that small house in Peoria, Illinois; I had two brothers and one sister. I was the only one in the family with enough courage to leave Illinois. The others seemed content to live out their lives there, but I ran off to California as soon as I could afford the ticket.

Los Angeles offered an escape from my outer circumstances, but not the inner torment I felt. At first I tried to insert myself into the circles that might help me break away from my Midwestern neurosis, but I was so much more comfortable on my own, holing away in my small apartment writing short stories and essays. Luckily my self-imposed exile paid off professionally and within two years I had a fair number of articles that had been published in respectable journals. Then a book proposal I sent to a small publisher was accepted, and before I knew it I was on my way.

I had already written two books by the time we met, neither of which were huge commercial successes. They did attain what one could call "cult status," which meant that the handful of people who actually did read them were fanatically loyal. Carolyn was one of those people, though in a way that was immensely refreshing. Being a successful artist in L.A. meant that she interfaced with celebrities much more recognizable than me, which left her completely unimpressed by my limited degree of fame. I received a message from a friend that a young, attractive woman wanted to meet me, and though I would normally never return such a call, I somehow felt compelled. More than once I had broken this rule, normally with embarrassing results. After all, this was forty years ago, 1959, and things were so much different then. I had never been married and my freedom brought with it a special kind of rebellion. This situation was different somehow, and I knew it. I decided to trust my instinct and see where it might lead.

The day I walked into the restaurant at the corner of Wilshire and Normandy changed my life. She said to look for the woman wearing a red headband sitting in a corner booth. I entered through the front door and scanned the room, waiting for someone to notice me. My habit was to remain a bit aloof and let whomever it is I was meeting see me first. But when our eyes finally met all that vanity disappeared and I felt my soul leap forward. Her eyes were like radiating pools of light and they seemed to pull me forward. And yet, there was nothing that could match the smile I saw. It was the sort of smile that was more a window to the soul, a soul brimming with life. I was captivated by her at once, and that captivation has continued now for forty years.

"Hi Fredrick, I'm Carolyn," she had said as she stood up from behind the booth.

"Hi, it's great to meet you. I'm Fred James, but I guess you already. . . ."

"Of course I know, I called you, remember?"

And that was how it all began. We sat in that

restaurant for hours talking and laughing, then decided to drive to Santa Monica to walk by the beach. I remember thinking that she was the most beautiful woman I had ever met, with her short black hair and open smile. Every time she looked at me I felt my knees go weak, and every smile was like a nail in my coffin. I wanted to reach out and touch her skin, or her hair, or even the air around her body. Anything would have satisfied me. I tried to resist the urge, to stay a safe distance away from her and not reveal more than I had to. But the feeling was becoming too strong. A tornado was turning inside me, and I didn't know how long I would be able to stay rooted in the place where I stood. I was falling for her like I had never fallen before, and the need for silence became apparent all too soon.

That night we were sitting together on a long pier looking out over the quiet ocean, and I felt as if my heart was speaking to me.

"She's the one," it whispered. "She's the one who can unravel all the chains you've wrapped around yourself. There's an energy that's moving between you that no one can fully comprehend, especially you, not yet anyway. Don't hold back this time, Fred. Open the door that you've hidden behind all these years, if only for a moment. She won't let you down, no matter how things appear at first."

She must have sensed what I was feeling. She turned away from me and looked out over the ocean, and I suddenly knew what she was thinking.

"This has been an incredible day, Fredrick, and I feel so fortunate to have met you, and to feel this connected to you." Then she looked at me and smiled. "We're going to be friends for a very long time, aren't we?"

"Yes, we are," I said, and it was all either one of us needed to say. We're going to be great friends. Hide it away now. Don't let her see how wide you've opened yourself. Go back to your room and learn not to trust the voice that doesn't know anything at all. "We're going to be very good friends," I said again beneath my breath.

I was thirty years old in 1960, and Carolyn was twenty-five. She had just moved to Hancock Park in Los Angeles two weeks earlier, renting a small bungalow behind a stately mansion that blocked her view of the quiet street. She became my best friend in less than a year, and I learned to hide the deeper pulse of my love behind a façade of thick branches and an impenetrable stone wall. The long walks we took through that neighborhood are still etched in my memory like thousand-year-old drawings upon a cave wall. I visit that cave in my mind as often as I can now, especially the day we first saw you, the Proposing Tree.

"Have you ever seen a more beautiful tree than this?" I remember her asking me. "It seems out of place here in the middle of Los Angeles, like it should be in the center of some small New England town, towering above all the old Victorian houses on Main Street. I'll bet it's older than every house in this neighborhood, and they built around it because it has some kind of special magic."

How could she have known what she was saying? Even you were unaware of the magic you held, and perhaps it took her words to release the alchemy. Regardless of how it happened, the moment we sat down beneath your shelter something moved in us both, though it has taken over thirty years for us to claim it.

We all plant seeds in the ground, but we must learn to patiently wait before we finally enjoy the fruit. A tree cannot grow overnight, and the more patient we are the deeper the roots sink into the earth. To rush the season is to miss the sweetness it could bear, and the life that should have been ours is then lost. You kept us from running too fast toward what we did not understand. And now that the harvest is full we feel the blessing you held. How can I express my gratitude to you, Great Tree?

"I have this dream of being proposed to beneath a tree like this," Carolyn said to me the first time she leaned against your trunk, letting her eyes move between the thick branches. "Especially on a day like this with a gentle breeze and a blue sky."

I stood next to her, just as I was prone to do, and reached out for her hand. "I've never really thought about it, but you're right. If I were to propose to a woman this would be the right place."

"Why don't you practice on me," she said as she spun around.

"What do you mean?" I asked, nervous and off balance.

"Let's practice on each other. You practice proposing and I'll practice saying 'Yes.' That way, when it's the real thing, we'll know what to do, how to look, everything. Come on, you're the writer, let your creative juices out and see what happens. It's best to be prepared for a moment like this. When you meet the right girl you can bring her here and you'll already know what to say."

"And what about you?" I asked.

"Well, my part is easy. I just have to look into his eyes adoringly and say, 'Yes, of course my darling, I'll marry you.' You're the one who has the hard part. One false word and the whole effect is lost."

She didn't catch what I was really asking her, and it was better that way. I was never able to do more than drop hints about my real feelings since I wasn't prepared to take the risk of losing her altogether. What I wanted to say was: "And if I really mean what I say, if the words that come from my mouth are true and my proposal is real, what will you do then?" But this was not the game she wanted to play. It was too real, too risky, and we both knew it. If I wanted to keep her, I would have to play by her rules, but by then I was already accustomed to this.

"Propose to me," she cried again as we stood next to you, Great Tree. "This might be your big chance, you shouldn't let an opportunity like this pass you by."

There was something about the way she said those words that stirred my soul, a deep place that hadn't existed a moment before. I looked into her eyes and saw every promise I had ever wrapped my heart around. Just for a moment I felt as if I were free, and the passion I had pushed down suddenly sprung forward and took a deep gulp of air.

"Please propose to me," she said again. "I promise to pretend it's real, as if you're the one I've searched for my whole life, as if you're the one I will give my heart and soul to for as long as we both shall live, and I promise not to laugh."

I didn't hear all the words she said. All I heard was, "You're the one I've searched for my whole life," and my heart began to sing out loud as I reached for her hand and fell to one knee.

"Beloved one, my heart overflows with a feeling my mind could never comprehend. The moment we met I died, only to be reborn again when you reached out and rescued my life. Every moment in your grace has been like a lifetime of loving, and I've completely forgotten what the world was like before you came. I've forgotten who I am, what my name is, or where I belong when I'm not in your arms. It's more than I can bear, Dearest, to look in the direction where you are not. I'm content to not move at all, but to hold perfectly still until we are joined in the Heavenly embrace that knows nothing of time, nothing of separation, and nothing of the space that exists between these earthly forms.

"So until the hour of our ascent comes, I ask but one favor, Beloved. Let me hold you in my arms for all time. It's the only thing that will ever satisfy me, the only thing that can set me free from this bondage. Marry me, Carolyn. Say you'll be my wife now and forever."

There was a long pause, as if the whole world held still waiting for her response. The words flew from my mouth so fast that there was nothing I could do to dissuade them from their destined mark. Had I said too much? Did I show her more blood than I intended? Our eyes were locked together and I swore I would never breathe again if she didn't answer soon.

"Wow," she finally sighed. "That was quite a proposal. Some woman is going to be thrilled by that one. You'll have to write it down so you can remember every word."

I let go of her hand and took a step backward, forcing a smile. "You think so?" I said to her, hiding my heart again. "I'm sure there's room for improvement."

"There's always room for improvement," she said. "But that's what I'm here for, to help you. Wait a minute, I forgot my part, didn't I? 'Yes, my beloved. I will marry you.'"

She threw her arms around me as if she had done so a thousand times before, and for just a moment I forgot my pain. At least I said it, I thought to myself. At least I said the words, though she never really heard them.

It became our ritual, the first thing we did whenever I visited Carolyn, and it continued for many years. I sometimes wondered what magic you held in your branches, Great Tree, that inspired such reverence, and what it was about her that needed the fantasy. Men entered her life then left, normally because she became bored, or because they held none of the promise she craved. I was the only person she brought to the Proposing Tree. No matter how close she grew to any of those others, this was like our sacrament, and it could never be shared with the uninitiated.

I want you to remember what she was like those first days. The early 60s were like a crease in time, as if we were suddenly forced from the Garden of Eden, but had yet to enter the Promised Land of the Beatles, free love, and hallucinogens. I was never particularly tempted by these extracurriculars, but Carolyn dove into them all with complete abandon. I began to see a side of her personality that worried my better intentions. Her inability to form a romantic partnership seemed to parallel her need to escape from the tangible world. I began to think that I was her distraction, giving her deeper feelings an outlet while maintaining a comfortable distance that let her bury who she really was.

She had been raised in a small, easily forgotten town in eastern Nebraska, the kind of town that spits out free spirits like Carolyn. She would have never survived in such a cage. She dreamed of becoming a great artist in New York, or sailing to London or Paris to live the life of a modern bohemian. Los Angeles was a safer option since she had one or two friends who had already made safe transitions. She stepped off the bus and began building a life for herself. Luckily her talent was considerable, and it didn't take long for her to get a respectable showing, then a long list of commissions. Success came naturally to her, while love was an uninvited guest.

By the time we met she was a rising star in the L.A. art community, and I, as mentioned before, was a kind of strange literary anomaly. My constant touring was a convenient distraction from my own inadequacies, and I was prone to a hermit-like seclusion whenever I was in town long enough to hold still. I would often lock myself away for days, sometimes for weeks, crafting what was sure to be my great breakthrough project. To say I was an overachiever would be an understatement, but my laser-like focus on whatever I was writing at the time kept life from creeping in on me. We were both afraid of really committing ourselves to life, and this, it turned out, made us strange allies.

But all these distractions disappeared whenever we stood here, beneath your branches, proclaiming our undying devotion to the ghostly mists of our future mates. I could feel her holding an etheric veil in front of my face, then projecting onto that veil every quality she thought she wanted in a man. She would hear his voice, whoever he was, saying all the things that only I could say, the fluid verse that came so easily because I meant every word. To her it was a play, and we were like actors on a stage. But for me it was something far more essential, far more real than the costumes and masks she would have me wear. I was in love with her. Every word I spoke beneath your branches was true, Great Tree, and every proposal was an undisguised overture meant to inspire a whole symphony of love.

"There is only one remedy that will revive my senses," I said to her once as you listened. "An unending kiss upon lips that never separate. Such sweetness would restore the years that were lived away from you, and return to me the vigor of my spoiled and scattered youth. The declarations that were nonsense to me once appear now as the balm that would save me from my despair. If you would but hear the angel that lies behind my stuttering words, then you would know how I long to enfold you in the blanket of my life.

"You search for love with the same abandon as I, but your eyes have been closed to my sacred vigil. Open them now and see who it is that stands with weighted feet and wings that long to fly. I will wait as long as you need, my beloved, wait until you answer me, until you say that you will marry me. For that, dear Carolyn, is the only thing that can save me now."

And she would stare into my eyes and I would wonder if she really understood. Then suddenly the veil would fall and she would retreat to the world of safe reflections, back to the cloud of sleep where we had both learned to hide from love. She would commend me on my brilliant proposal and I would feign modesty. I was too afraid to risk everything, to tell her the truth without the camouflage of your branches. This slow approach was better than losing her, and I learned to be content with the charade.

But then one day all that changed.

"I believe that the universe has reserved someone for me," she said to me as we sat beneath your branches in 1963. "There's someone out there who I have yet to meet sitting beneath a tree much like this one thinking about me, wondering where I am. There was a seed that Heaven planted in both of our souls, and we'll never be content until we find one another. Maybe we were together before we were born, and we made a serious pact to find one another here. Sometimes I think I see him in my dreams, and I can feel myself reaching out for his hand. But then I wake up feeling lonelier than ever before. What do you think, Fredrick? Do you think any of that is possible?"

I remember the way I stopped myself from saying what I really felt. I wanted to proclaim the journey over, to shake her where she sat and demand she open her eyes. The feeling only lasted a second, and then I regained my practiced composure. I said something that neither one of us expected.

"What if there's more than one person for us, like a soul group and each person searches for the others. Maybe you have more than one soul partner, different relationships that transcend the normal boundaries of intimacy and romance. It could be another woman, or I might meet another man, and it would have nothing to do with sex or physical partnering."

"I'm not sure I'm following you," she said. "You think that we may have more than one soul partner, and it may not have anything to do with romance?"

"I don't know where the idea came from, but yes. What if one of those people is right in front of you and the circumstances of your life make you blind, so you keep searching for someone else? And what if that person is one of many, and that around the corner there are others who will make just as strong of an impact on your life?"

I could feel myself stretching further out onto the limb, and it was beginning to crack behind me. There was a look on her face that I dreaded, as if she were climbing inside my heart and didn't like what she saw. I could feel her spirit retracting, much as she had done the first night we met when she decided to lay the ground rules for our involvement. I had never dared test those boundaries, and without realizing it I was suddenly walking down an uncharted street.

"What are you trying to say to me? Hopefully not what I think you're saying."

Where was I going? I searched for the emergency brake but my hand fumbled and my foot hit the accelerator. Before I knew it I was racing toward certain demise. All those unheard, unfelt proposals suddenly rushed in around me, and I felt a strange mixture of resentment and exhilaration. How could she sit there year after year without realizing that all those proposals were real? I meant every word, while to her it was just a game. In that moment I didn't care what she thought, and I didn't care if she was afraid of me. Maybe that's what we both needed, to confront the issue once and for all.

"There's something I want to tell you," I said to Carolyn. "I've lost track of how many times I've seen you enter a room, and then no matter what everyone's doing, everything stops and they all turn to watch you. All you have to do is smile and the whole world lights up, and you never even seem to realize it. Maybe that's part of your charm, your inability to see the impact you have on others. And then I notice my own response, the way I feel when I watch everyone notice you. I feel proud, proud to know that you're about to walk up to me and take my hand, and just for a moment everyone in the room thinks we're together. But it's not the kind of pride one feels for a friend, Carolyn, and that's what makes it feel so awkward. It's the kind of pride a husband feels for his wife. But then I remember that you're not my wife, and never will be. And I just stand there with this strange feeling filling my chest, holding your hand and watching the whole room think I must be very special indeed."

"That's one of the sweetest things anyone has ever said to me," she said, surprising me. "But I want to look at it a bit deeper. I'm glad you feel proud, but it scares me when you say that because I think you're waiting for me to change the way I feel."

"I'm not waiting for you to change anything," I said, trying to retreat.

"Then what are you doing? I love you, Fredrick, but you're not 'The One,' and we both know it. It would have shifted on its own if you were. I need you to be realistic and not harbor fantasies."

I had come too far to turn back. To stop there would have been like castrating myself. She was going to hear the whole truth whether she wanted to or not. Even if it meant losing her forever, for the first time it was a chance I was willing to take.

"Carolyn, I don't want you to feel uncomfortable, but I can't deny what's real for me. You see . . . sometimes I forget that I'm not in love with you. Sometimes I forget that you will never feel the love I feel. It's that simple, and that tragic."

She stood up and towered over me. "Sometimes you forget you're not in love with me? Why don't you add that line to your repertoire, because it's very moving? You know, the thing that's most important to me is respect, and you're not respecting my feelings, feelings that I've been very clear about since we met. Maybe this tree is starting to get to you or something, but it's not going to work."

I stood up and faced her. "What are you so afraid of, Carolyn? You run from everything. Are you going to run from me now? For once in your life stand still and face the darkness that hovers around you."

"What are you saying to me? Who are you to tell me to face my darkness? You sit in your room for weeks at a time doing God-knows-what, and you have the nerve to tell me to stop running? You're the one with running shoes on, my friend. Or maybe you're not my friend after all. If this is the way you show how much you care for me, then you can shove it."

She started to storm away, and just before she left your shadow she turned back and faced me one last time. "And you can shove all your proposals as well. I don't ever want to come here with you again. Sit here by yourself for awhile and see how it feels."

Then she walked away, and I was alone. I don't remember if I cried in front of you or not, Great Tree. Perhaps you can remember for me, especially now that so much has changed. You are so much older than I am, even though my eyesight fails me now and even my memories are like clouds. I do remember that I sat here for a very long time, and you never moved at all.

Three years passed before I saw Carolyn again. I never once came to see you during that period, and I even tried to forget what it felt like to sit beneath your branches. Too many dreams had been shattered here and I didn't want all those meaningless proposals to flood into my mind again. I tried to push them away, to act as if Carolyn was just a passing phase in my life. If she had not made the next move, I may have actually succeeded.

I finally wrote the breakthrough novel I dreamed of, and before I knew it I was on every best-seller list in the country. It was near the end of a whirlwind book tour and I was giving a lecture at a major L.A.

bookstore when everything changed. I looked out and saw her sitting in the audience. Our eyes locked and she flashed the smile that had won my heart so many years before. It was hard to focus on what I was there to say, and I felt a wave of relief when it was finally time to end.

I was signing books at the table that had been set up for the occasion and I scanned the crowd hoping she hadn't left. Don't come this close and then turn away, I thought to myself. I would do anything to go back to the way it was before, to forget all the things I said and pretend they weren't real. I let my heart slip away from me and it has cost us so much. I've paid for my mistake, three long years of trying to forget. You can forget the tree and the proposals if you want, but don't forget me.

"Hello, Fredrick." The voice came from behind me and I spun around to face her. We didn't dare touch each other, as if we were waiting for a sign that would say everything was forgiven.

"Carolyn, I can't believe you're here. What are you—"

"How could I stay away?" she said. "Look what you've done . . . exactly what you wanted. Now it's me who's proud of you."

I bowed my head as if I didn't want to hear those words. But it felt good, and I was happy she was there.

"What are you doing? Can we go out after I'm done here?"

"Take your time. I can wait."

It was nearly Christmas and the streets were filled with flashing lights and decorations. We walked down Melrose and looked into the shop windows, never once touching hands or brushing up against one another. Some of the stores had holiday music playing and it helped lighten the tense air. I was so glad to see her, but we both hesitated in showing it. What did she want me to do, reach out and take her arm and tell her how sorry I was? I would have gladly done it, but my fear stopped me.

"I have something I want to say to you." It was Carolyn who broke the silence, and I was glad for it. "It was wrong for me to react the way I did when you shared your feelings three years ago. You were right, I was running. I was afraid of love and of losing the most important person in my life—you. In a way it was the best thing that could happen to me, because it shook me to my core. I had to wake up and take a hard look at who I am . . . who I was, I mean. It wasn't a pretty picture, but I believed I could change. What you said helped me, but I was afraid that you would never forgive me the things I said to you. That's why I didn't find you till now. It finally got to the point that I couldn't hold back any longer. I had to see you, no matter what your reaction was."

"I feel the same way," I said to her, finally reaching out for her hand. "You are my dearest friend, and I don't think I could have gone on much longer without you. I saw an article about you around a year ago, an announcement for a gallery opening. I wanted to come but something stopped me. We both were afraid of one thing or another, but we can't let it stop us, not even for a moment. We've already wasted too much time."

Everything shifted and suddenly it was as if nothing had ever changed. We talked and laughed like we used to and realized that the bond had not been broken at all. I forgot about the way I jumped forward and frightened her, and she released the guilt she felt for walking away. I had my friend back, and just in time for Christmas.

I drove her home that night, back to the bungalow where she had lived for years. "Turn here," she said when we were a few blocks away. I knew where she was taking me, back to you, the Proposing Tree. At first I was afraid, but it all disappeared when she reached out and took hold of my hand. I turned the corner and saw you were covered with tiny white lights, and my heart began to sing again.

"I come here almost every night," she said to me. "It's always so beautiful this time of year. I wanted to come with you, to sit beneath the tree again. And maybe even . . ."

"Don't tell me you want me to . . ."

"I won't ask you to do anything that makes you feel uncomfortable. But it would make me so happy to hear you say the words. No one can propose quite as well as you."

We parked the car and walked to the very spot where I am writing these words. I have never been lucky enough to have what felt like a real home. My family split apart when I was young and I never found much peace in the world. But in that moment I felt like I had found the home I never had. Sitting here beneath your branches with Carolyn at my side has been the greatest pleasure of my life, and I will remember it for as long as I live.

"Open your heart to me, Fredrick," she said as she took my hand and looked into my eyes. "I promise that I will honor your words, and I will never run from you again. Propose to me as if I'm the one you've been waiting for, as if I'm the answer to your deepest dream."

I took a deep breath and opened the door one more time. The well was still there where I left it, the reservoir of light that had inspired me years earlier. I let the bucket of my conscious mind fall into that deep hole and began pulling words and feelings from that dark place that I had wanted to forget. But I couldn't forget them, and I didn't really want to. Whether she heard my prayer or not she was standing there, and I was willing to love again.

"Beloved Carolyn, my love for you knows no limitation, and no earthly care can intrude upon the holiness you have shown me. I could feel angel wings brush against my face the first time I heard your voice, and since then I have learned to sing just as they sing, to ascend the heightened scales that no human voice can ever hear. How could I bear to stand at your side if not for the grace these angels have showered upon us both, or without singing the song that fills their ears even now?

"And yet, I would lay all these heavenly encounters aside if you would but grant me one favor. There is nothing either in this world nor the world to come that can satisfy the urge to love you with my whole life, my whole soul, and every quickened beat of my heart. It will race forever if you do not extend to me this one gift, the gift of your hand in marriage. Only then will I breathe deeply again, for I have grown accustomed to tightening my lungs in case you turn from me. Accept me this and every moment, Beloved Carolyn, and I will sing again, and the angels will rejoice."

She closed her eyes and tears began to roll off her cheeks onto the ground. "Yes," she said to me. "You're going to make some woman very happy someday, just as happy as you've made me tonight."

Chapter Two

Another three years passed, and without realizing it we fell into a comfortable rhythm that was almost marital, though without the intimacies normally associated with the sacrament. I found myself spending the night at her apartment more than at my own. The black couch in the corner of her living room was deceptively comfortable and it consoled my spirit as well as my body. We spent most days together in Carolyn's studio. She painted and I sat in the corner scribbling notes that would someday fill the pages of a book I promised to write. All in all it was one of the happiest times of my life. We never talked about my deeper feelings, though they never receded far from my mind, even for a day. Carolyn seemed to accept them though, as if they were a comfort to her during the long periods when no other men came to call. We loved each other in a way that we didn't expect, but it was natural nonetheless.

It had always been Carolyn's dream to see London, and so I invited her to join me on a publicity tour, then spend a week touring the countryside. Planning the trip was in itself an exciting event. I had never seen her so free and childlike, and it eased the cynical side of my own personality that dreaded these trips. We were closer than we had ever been before, and for the first time in my life I felt what seemed to approach contentment.

At the last minute a lecture had been scheduled at a church in London a day after we arrived. Carolyn whined nearly the entire flight because it would encroach upon the free time we had set aside to wander wherever the cool English wind blew us. I convinced her that it was only one day, and that I wouldn't allow any other distractions. Then she fell asleep with her head on my shoulder, and my mind began to consider fantasies that I normally would never allow. I took out my notepad and wrote these words, trying hard not to wake her:

"This is my wife, the woman I care for above every

other. There is nothing I would not do for her, nothing that could impose upon my devotion. If she were to call to me from the other side of the world I would find a way to be with her. If she were to test me with some fanciful whim just to see how I would respond, I would run to her side and fulfill her every demand. Such a stance could never intrude upon my masculinity as some might think, for I feel more a man when I am serving her than when I am not. I am her protector, her shield against the cold winds of the unforgiving world. The more she asks of me the more I receive from her, and this fulfills my desire in a way that no passerby can understand.

"No man-made indulgence can satisfy me the way she does. Heaven alone rivals her radiance and her kiss surely leads to those passionate gates. Where else would she have me go but from her arms into the arms of the Divine? She passes me into that angelic realm with such grace that I cannot tell where she ends and where God begins. They are the same to me now, and I could never choose which I prefer. She taught me how to wrap myself around two worlds, one with her and the other so subtle that we disappear together in that light, held tight in the embrace which even the angels envy."

"How long have I been asleep?" she asked as she shattered the rhythm of my imagination. I closed the pad and placed it in the seat pocket in front of me.

"Maybe an hour," I told her. "Were you dreaming?"

"Yes, I was," she said as she sat up straight. "You and I were walking together in a field on this glorious day. In the distance we could see someone, a man, though I don't think I knew who he was. He was calling to both of us and trying to catch up to where we were. He was starting to get close and I was almost able to see his face . . . then I woke up. What do you think it means?"

"I'm not very good at interpreting dreams," I said to her. "Maybe it doesn't mean anything at all."

"Oh, it does . . . I can feel it. It was a premonition of some sort. I've had them before, and they always mean something."

And that was all that was said about the dream. I have to admit that at the moment I didn't think much about it at all, but within days all that changed. I realize now what I could not have known then—that the tumblers of the universe were shifting, and the door that opened to a world we shared alone was now gone. Her vision was more than an unconscious glimpse into a possible world, but an advance screening of an event that was about to change both our lives.

How Carolyn loved England. The gypsy soul she had denied all her life rose like the Tower of London and sang in a way that astounded us both. Why did we wait so long to leave the familiar trappings of our lives to adventure out into these new worlds? I began to think that the sudden change in air might open more than her spirit, but her heart as well. If she could see all these ancient buildings and hills with fresh eyes, maybe she could turn toward me and perceive the love I had worn like a ring, but hidden all those forgotten years. And if she could see this ring and call it to the surface of my life, would it not breathe for the first time, long deep breaths that would awaken us both? These thoughts and dreams filled my soul as we walked along the Thames that first night in London, and I actually thought we were about to soar above the old forms that we had grown so used to.

"I have been thinking about soul-partners," she said to me as we walked along the bank of that sleepy river. "I remember talking to you about it once before and you said that maybe we are reserved for more than one person, that there could be whole groups of people waiting and searching for one another."

"Yes, I do remember that," I said, only half paying attention.

"Why do you think we were drawn together again? You're more important to me than anyone I have ever met, Fredrick, and yet I have the feeling that there are more out there waiting for us. I have been having so many dreams lately that I can't really explain, but they give me the feeling that something's about to happen, something big."

"What do you think it is?" I asked her, my interest suddenly awakened.

"The dream I told you about . . . the one about seeing another man who I seem to know . . . it wasn't the first time I had that dream. It's always the same . . . you and I are together and there's another man trying to catch us. And the feeling I get when I see him is amazing, like we've been looking for him our entire lives. And yet he can never get close. Every time he does I wake up and he's gone. Just the feeling remains."

I remember feeling threatened by Carolyn's dream. Even if it was just a coincidence, it meant that she was more focused on an illusion than she was on me. It was a personal grudge I held against her, the feeling that she was unable to see what was right in front of her. There I was, holding a passion I could barely contain, and yet she looked past me every time, more attuned to a shadow than to a real, breathing man she could reach out and touch, perhaps even hold and love.

The next night we traveled by limousine to St. James Church in Piccadilly, where I was scheduled to speak to around 300 people. My last book had just reached the best-seller list in England and expectations were high. The Brits, after all, are a whole different audience to a Yank like me. The well-rehearsed jokes that go over so well in the States sink like a lead weight in England. Then there is the usual prejudice to overcome, the idea that all Americans are loud and overdone. It was the third time I had been invited to tour the UK, and luckily I had already learned the ropes. We walked in through the back of the church at exactly seven and the audience was already filled. There wasn't a single person who arrived late. How very English, I remember thinking to myself.

Carolyn sat in the back of the church while I walked toward the front. The crowd was tepid and polite when I stood at the altar and began my talk. Now and then they nodded appreciatively, as if they liked what they heard but had no intention of showing the kind of enthusiasm I was used to receiving. But I was prepared for this and even had a backup plan. My agent, who was himself English, had given me a few sure hits, the kind of jokes that only the English can appreciate. I have to admit that when my friend shared them with me I was hardly impressed, but just as he said they would, the audience roared with approval. I had broken through, and the rest was easy.

I don't remember what I said that night, Great Tree, for so many years have passed since that time. I do remember looking at Carolyn often, as if she were the source of all my energy. Now and then she would notice my glance and would send me a wide smile, the sort that always stopped my heart. I could see how proud she was of me, and that meant more than anything else. It helped me turn a respectable showing into one of the best talks I ever gave. Her presence made me want to excel, for to impress Carolyn was more important than conquering Europe. Her smile was more valuable to me than the Crown Jewels, even if the Queen presented them herself.

When the presentation was finished, I was expected to stand at a table to the side of the altar and sign books. This was the part of being an author I loved the most. The personal connection I felt with my readers made my solitary life feel worthwhile, as if the stories and ideas I shared were more than just my own, but were part of a greater whole that had the power to transform the world. I remember looking into their eyes and realizing how important my books were to their lives. It has been many years since I have written like that, since I felt that satisfaction, but the memory survives.

At one point I looked toward the back of the church and saw Carolyn talking to a young, very handsome man. He had long brown hair that fell over his shoulder and eyes that could melt any woman. I could also tell by the way Carolyn responded to him that she was more than a little affected by his charm. She would reach out and touch his arm often, something I had seen her do a thousand times before, then pull him into her own deep eyes, a trick she had mastered. I could feel myself becoming agitated, but there was nothing I could do about it until the last person in line had the chance to say hello and got her book signed.

The church was nearly deserted when I finally had the opportunity to leave the table and go to where Carolyn stood talking to the young man. As I approached them I realized that he was better looking than I first thought. His clothes also made him stand out in the crowd, the kind of wardrobe I often saw in the more artistic neighborhoods in New York. When he saw me coming he seemed genuinely anxious to say hello. I, on the other hand, placed a wall between us, something I am ashamed of now, for at that moment he was nothing more than a competitor, another cute hippie bent on stealing the woman I had devoted my life to loving.

"Mr. James, it is an honor to meet you," he said as he extended his hand. His handshake was firm, but not too firm, the sort of handshake a man enjoys receiving from another man. "I must say that I thoroughly enjoyed your presentation."

"Fredrick, this is Colin Church," Carolyn said before I had the chance to say a word. "He is a musician here in Britain, and will soon be touring in the States as well. He's read all of your books."

"Yes, I am a bit embarrassed to admit that I'm always the first to our local seller whenever one comes to print. You are a great writer, and I'm thrilled to finally meet you in person."

"What kind of music do you do?" I asked him, more out of politeness than interest.

"He's a big rock star," Carolyn said as she reached for his arm again. "He's part of the British Invasion, you know, like the Beatles and the Rolling Stones." Then she turned toward Colin. "Fredrick's not into music much, unless it's classical. Then you can't keep him away."

I could see a confused look in Colin's eyes, as if he were trying to discern whether Carolyn and I were romantic or not. She had obviously explained that we were together, but the way she hung on his every word made it appear that we were just friends. Maybe he thought I was gay, and that Carolyn and I were traveling companions. I wish I had asked him that question, especially now that he is gone. I would like to have known what he was thinking that first night. Instead I am left to guess, drawing upon incomplete information to understand the man that meant more to me than any other.

"I've been watching you two from the front for nearly an hour," I said with a hint of sarcasm. "I was beginning to wonder . . ."

"Oh, don't start, Fredrick," Carolyn said with her usual lilt. "Colin has been a complete gentleman . . .

but I must admit that his accent is beginning to get to me."

That was the line I was waiting for. It was Carolyn's way of saying, "Just so you know, Fredrick and I are just friends . . . that's all. Make your move if you dare." Colin, on the other hand, seemed too refined to take the bait, as if he was completely aware of what was happening but wasn't going to fall backwards into her trap. Carolyn seemed to sense this and stepped back slightly.

"Well, I'm sure you both have better things to do than stand here all night talking to me," Colin said. "It has been a pleasure meeting you both."

"We were just about to find a restaurant and get something to eat," I said before I realized it. "Maybe you could join us?"

Colin looked at us both as if judging his response from the look in our eyes. "Yes, actually I would love to join you. I know of a few good restaurants in this neighborhood and would be honored if you would be my guests."

And that was how it started. It's hard to believe that so many years have passed and that he has been gone so long. I am an old man now and have been honored by the presence of so many dear friends, so many comrades that have come and gone in my life. But none ever matched the love I felt for Colin. By the time we finished that first meal I sensed a feeling of tenderness for him that I have never felt for another man. It was organic, almost as if it were beyond my conscious self, but existed in another realm that we visit only in our dreams. Whatever it was I knew he would be with us for a very long time, and I could tell that Carolyn felt the same.

Over the next three days Carolyn and I toured London, and Colin was never far from our side. I had already forgotten the jealousy I felt when we met. In fact, I started to think I was more taken by him than Carolyn was. She had adopted a more distant stance than she had demonstrated the first night, and I started to wonder what had changed. On one hand, Colin was the perfect tour guide, and he was all too willing to share everything he knew about his city. On the other hand, the constant rush of fans clamoring for his autograph was distracting, and it was becoming hard for us to relax and enjoy one another's company.

I sometimes wonder what it was about Colin that drew me so. He was like the brother I never had, though even that wasn't true. I had two biological brothers, but they never entered my soul as deeply as Colin. Perhaps I was craving a connection I knew I would never get from Carolyn, for he was her masculine mirror in so many ways. Decades have passed since we met, and yet no man ever touched me as he did. I have given up trying to understand what it means or why it happened. All I know is that the three of us were meant to be together, though it was so fleeting and shifted so fast.

Later that night when Carolyn and I were alone at the hotel I could sense that something was wrong. She was more distant than normal and didn't seem open to me at all. At first I didn't say anything to her, which is my normal inclination. If someone's not willing to share what's eating them, then I'm not accustomed to prying it loose. But with Carolyn this never lasted long. I could never stand for there to be a river between us that I knew I could bridge. When we were settled in our room I opened up the door of her heart to have a look.

"Why don't you just admit what you're trying to do?" she said to me in a cold voice.

"What do you . . ."

"Don't play that game with me, Fredrick. You know very well what I mean. You don't want Colin to open up to me so you're hogging him for yourself. You hardly even let me get a word in. All that nonsense the two of you talk about. It's all just a game to you—keep him looking one direction so he doesn't wander very far away."

"What are you talking about?" I objected. "I have no intention of keeping the two of you apart. In fact, of all the men you've met in the last few years, I like him the best. If anything, I would encourage you getting to know him."

"That's not true and you know it. Any man that comes into my life, especially Colin, threatens you. It's your subtle way of keeping me to yourself, even though you know very well where we stand. Fredrick, you're my friend, and that's all. When are you going to . . ."

That was all I heard, though her tirade continued on for some time. I didn't want to hear those words, those cutting daggers that knew the path to my heart all too well. Better to block their path and not let them near my awareness. Better to close off completely and hear what soothes my spirit, though those words were not heard at all in those days. I wanted her to speak to me the way she wanted to speak to Colin, not with words that destroy. I wanted her to say that she loved me, and that she wanted to reach out toward my life with arms that heal. I would have to wait many years to hear words like that.

The next morning I woke up alone. Carolyn was gone and there was no sign of her luggage or clothes anywhere. I ran out of the hotel and looked up and down the street hoping to find her. Once or twice I thought I caught a glimpse, but then it vanished like a ghost in the crowd. After an hour I walked back to the hotel and tried to decide what to do.

When I got to the lobby I saw Colin sitting in a large red chair near the entrance. He stood up when he saw me and walked toward the door.

"Fredrick, I'm glad you're here. Carolyn is at my house. She called late last night and said she had to leave. She was drunk and wasn't making much sense, so I sent a mini to pick her up. She slept on the couch, and as far as I know she's still there."

"Why are you here?" I asked him. "Why didn't you stay with her?"

"Because I need to talk to you alone," he said. "I feel I can say things to you that I can't say to Carolyn. I want to be straight and ask you a few questions if you don't mind."

I told him to go ahead.

"First of all, I need to know what your relationship is with Carolyn. Are you lovers, or involved romantically?"

I didn't want to answer him. I was angry that he left her alone when she was in such a state, then came to me with such questions. I wanted to tell him to leave and never come back. I wanted to tell him that we were engaged, or were lovers, or whatever else would keep him away. There were so many things that I wanted to say, but I didn't say any of them. I sensed his sincerity and felt at that moment that I loved him just as Carolyn seemed to love him.

"No, we're not," I said. "We're just friends, very good friends."

Colin seemed relieved and sat down in a nearby chair. I followed and sat down beside him.

"I've never felt this way before," he said as he stared at the floor. "I've never met a woman like Carolyn, and I think I'm the one who is falling in love with her. But I'm not like you Fredrick. I'm not good with words, unless I'm singing them, of course. But even then someone else has to write them. I don't know what to say. If I try I'm sure to stumble and embarrass myself."

"Are you telling me that you're afraid to tell her how you feel?" I asked.

"Afraid . . . unable . . . it's all the same for me. I've always been this way. People think that because I'm a musician that I should be good at romance. Most of my colleagues sleep with every woman they meet, but I'm not like that. I also don't know how to . . . how to express myself. Maybe you could help me. For you it's so easy. That's why I love your books. Words flow from you like . . ."

"Like incense from a hot coal?" I said.

"Yes . . . you see, even when you're talking to me you're brilliant."

"Colin, I appreciate what you're saying, but I don't think I can help you. You see . . ."

"Please, Fredrick," he pleaded. "I'll be touring the States in a few weeks and can spend some time with you and Carolyn in L.A. You don't know what this means to me. I don't care how you do it, but you must. . . ."

I don't know why I ended up agreeing to such a preposterous idea. After all, this was Carolyn he was talking about, the woman I loved. But it was also becoming clear that I loved Colin as well, and that I would do anything for him, including to help him secure the affection of the woman I would sacrifice everything for. I spent the rest of the day in complete turmoil, wondering if I had lost my mind. Then

Carolyn returned to the hotel and we made things right between us. I didn't say anything about my conversation with Colin. If I were to actually follow through on my promise, it would have to be in my own time.

Something had changed between Carolyn and me, though I was not able to pinpoint what it was or how it happened. The intimacy we shared was slowly receding, as if she had to psychically pull away from me to create enough room for Colin to enter. Was this the man she saw in her dream, I wondered? If it was, then he was bound to impact my life as much as hers. All our talk about soul mates and soul-families was being played out in front of our eyes. The week we spent with Colin in England was magic, and neither of us could wait for him to arrive in the States. It was as if his spirit were being woven into the fabric of both our lives, and we were overjoyed to have him there.

I didn't sleep at Carolyn's bungalow much before Colin arrived. It made it easier for both of us, I believe, as if we both knew that everything was about to change. Only I knew about Colin's feelings for her, and I wondered how it would all play out. He wanted me to help him . . . but how? Together we were like the perfect mate for Carolyn, him with his good looks and voice, and me with the words she longed to hear. If only we could become one person, one voice and face for her, then the whole universe would be right again. But it would never end like this. Only one man would finally have her, or so it seemed at that moment.

Colin's fame was sweeping across the country. Even before he arrived he had a single in the top ten and another one climbing the charts. It was hard to pass the magazine stand near my home and not see his face on the cover of at least one publication. He was destined to come to us as a star, and I knew that this would only complicate things further.

Carolyn could think of nothing else. In all the years I had known her I had never seen her so completely overwhelmed by a man. Had it not been for my own feelings for Colin I may have been destroyed. Somehow I was able to bear it. But how would I help him secure her love? It was clear what he wanted, to put my words into his mouth and pretend they were his own. Perhaps I would have been willing to make a trade, to step for a moment into his skin and see through his liquid eyes. And yet, I wasn't sure I wanted to play the role of matchmaker too soon.

"Fredrick, I need to talk to you," Carolyn said to me days before Colin arrived. "I've been trying to hide just how much he means to me, though we haven't even known each other very long. You seem to feel it as well . . . how special he is. That's why I know I need to talk about it, even though it may hurt you."

"It's not going to hurt me," I said, lying a bit. "You're right, Colin means a great deal to both of us. I feel like he's my brother, and if I was you I wouldn't waste any time. You must go to him."

"Never," she said as she stood up and turned away. "There are a few things I'm still a bit old fashioned about, and one of them is that I won't chase a man. If he wants me he has to ask, otherwise forget it." Her eyes caught fire and I could feel the heat from the other side of the room. "You don't understand how it is, Fredrick. If he feels it too, he'll do everything to make me love him. And if he doesn't, then nothing has been lost. But I'll never say a word."

I have to admit that I had never seen this side of Carolyn before, which seemed to indicate a level of seriousness that had not been present with any of the other men she had been with. But this put me in a rather difficult position. It meant that I needed to find a way to help Colin make the first move, if he could find the courage. I was beginning to plot how I would get him to say what he needed to say to win her heart. Maybe he could memorize the lines I gave him, but words without the proper delivery were doomed to fail. I was determined to find a way to wrap his tongue around the poetry that Carolyn loved. I wasn't going to fail, even though success meant that she would never be mine.

Colin arrived in L.A. like a dream. There was no way we could lead normal lives when we were with him. We couldn't go to restaurants or even shop. If we did he was sure to be mobbed, and that was certainly not the romance Carolyn was looking for. As soon as I had the chance, I had to get him alone so we could plan our strategy. We finally met at a local diner frequented by an older clientele. I figured no one would recognize him there.

"Have you decided to help me?" Colin asked. "Please say you have. . . . I haven't been able to concentrate on my tour for weeks now. The anticipation . . ."

"Yes, I'm going to help you," I said. "But we need to get a few things straight first. You have to find a way to say the right words to her, and if you can then everything will be perfect. That's one thing I know about Carolyn, she loves for a man to speak to her in the language of love. One way or another you need to get over your fear and talk to her about your feelings."

"But I can't do that . . . I already told you. Whenever I try, I fall over my own two feet, like a clown."

"You see, that was good. That was a witty way of saying how you feel. Why can't you do the same thing about your love?"

"Because it's different," he said. "I'm not afraid to talk to you. It's only when it's about love that I freeze, or when I'm with Carolyn. This is the first time I'm willing to confront that weakness, but with your help."

"I don't know," I said to him. "Carolyn is a very smart woman. If she finds out we planned this then it will be the end for both of us."

"I trust you, Fredrick. You're like a brother to me."

That was all he needed to say to get me in his corner. If I wasn't going to have her, then Colin would. In that moment my love for them both grew beyond measure. I knew that I was being asked to make the ultimate sacrifice, to surrender them both and step aside. And yet, if I had known how heavy the cost would be I may have never done it at all.

I could feel Carolyn and Colin growing closer as each day passed. My influence, on the other hand, was receding. Carolyn's dream seemed to be coming true.

Colin had been trying to catch up to us and he was nearly there. What would I do when he finally arrived? Could this amazing triad we created continue, or was it best for me to step back altogether so they could have a real chance at love. That consideration still seemed far away since nothing else mattered till Colin said "the words." Carolyn was resolute in her decision to not commit her feelings till he declared his own. I did what I could to break down this wall, but she wouldn't budge. It was obvious that she was in love with Colin, but her fear of intimacy and the possibility of being hurt made her hold back.

Colin seemed to have underestimated his inability to speak words of romance. There were so many opportunities he missed, opportunities I would have seized. He just didn't have the touch, though his heart was wide open. Whenever the moment was right and Carolyn sat in front of him waiting for him to declare himself, he would retreat into the safety of the mundane. I was beginning to wonder if it was a lost cause, and I knew that Carolyn was thinking the same thing.

Then one night Carolyn and I did something that we had never done before, and haven't done since.

We invited Colin to come with us to you, Proposing Tree, welcoming him to join us in the most blessed sacrament we knew. I could feel Carolyn fill with hope when we turned the corner and saw you there. You stood with your arms open wide as if to pull from our hearts those deeper moods that would inspire us in ways we didn't expect. If you could speak with words you would have told us what needed to happen, and you would have led us out of our imaginary world into the light. "Just trust . . ." that's what you were saying, and I heard you. As we crossed the street and stepped onto the sidewalk I knew that my life was about to change, and there was nothing I could do to stop it.

Carolyn stopped at your great trunk, then turned to face us. The golden rays of the moon illumined her face in a way I had never seen before, and her smile was as wide as the sky. In that moment I wanted to push Colin away from us and force Carolyn to face me. I wanted to take her by the arms and tell her again that every word I ever said beneath your branches was real, and that each proposal that came from my lips was but the herald of my deepest heart. Why was I being forced to turn every line over to this man, no matter how much I cared for him? How could they push me into this position, stealing from me the only things I had, my words and my heart?

Colin stood back for a moment and seemed to hesitate before stepping toward you. It was as if he knew what would happen, as if he were aware of the gift I was about to give. I was about to open my heart so that he could reflect the light that was held but for her, light that had been concealed in a secret room for many years waiting to be released. I was beginning to lose track of how many years I spent molding these moments, caressing the sacredness of a passion that Carolyn had yet to understand. And now three people stood at the crossroad, and I was all too aware of what would happen next.

"Should we tell him?" Carolyn asked.

Colin looked at us both as if he wasn't sure what to say.

"She means this tree," I said. "This is a very special tree to us, and you're the first person we've ever brought here. We call it the Proposing Tree, because it's where we practice saying those words that we all dream of saying to someone we love, or hearing the words that change everything forever. It's sort of a tradition or a ritual for us . . . it's been going on for years."

"Let me get this right," Colin said, as if he couldn't believe what he was hearing. "You propose to one another at this tree? But why? Maybe I'm too English and it's beyond my comprehension, but I find that absolutely amazing."

"It is amazing," Carolyn said to him, "and no one proposes marriage like Fredrick. It's amazing he's never been married. It's a shame really, all those remarkable proposals being wasted on me."

"Nothing has been wasted on you," I said to her, giving her another glimpse at my heart. "Nothing I ever said was wasted."

This caught her off guard; she wasn't expecting such an honest response. She looked at me for a moment as if the whole world suddenly disappeared, the street, Colin, everything but you, Great Tree. Carolyn and I were standing there looking at each other, and I'm sure that in some parallel universe it really happened. Somewhere, in another time perhaps, she reached out her hand and touched my face, as if the scales finally fell off her eyes and she recognized who was standing before her. But it was just a dream, a fantasy I wanted but which never existed at all. She blinked once and the effect was lost.

"One of the advantages to being a great writer," Colin said to me. "You have the ability to make women swoon."

"You do the same thing every time you sing," I said with a manufactured smile. "There are millions of women around the world who dream of you in their arms."

"Why don't the two of you be quiet and look around," Carolyn said as she wrapped her arms around the lower part of your trunk. "This is my favorite place on Earth. This is what romance is all about, having my two favorite men at my side standing here at this tree. If I place my ear to the trunk I can sense every proposal that has ever been spoken here. Time seems to be collapsing and everything is beginning to slow down. This is the place where only one thing matters—love. Come closer, both of you, and see if you can feel what I mean."

The moment had arrived. Only I knew what the next move would be. I had decided it was best that Colin be in the dark, completely oblivious to my plan. It was best not to give him too much time to think, otherwise he was sure to show signs of strain. Carolyn, of course, knew nothing. She had no idea that I was about to place the thing she wanted most in the world right in front of her. I was the only person standing there who knew anything at all.

"Carolyn," I said to her, "why don't we show Colin how we do it."

"You mean, you want to propose to me right now?"

"Why not? It would be wrong to bring him here without giving him the whole effect. We've done this dozens of times before and now, for the first time, we bring someone as a witness. It's perfect, and Colin is the only person in the world that either of us trusts with this sacred task."

Carolyn smiled as if she knew where I was leading her. I'm sure she thought that I was trying to set a good example for Colin. Maybe if he saw me do it then it wouldn't seem so hard, then he would be able to garner his courage and step forward on his own. There was no way for her to know what I really had in mind, that I intended to do something that neither one of them expected. How could she have realized how far I was willing to go?

"Maybe this is something I shouldn't see," Colin said. "After all . . ."

"You just stand here and watch," I said as I moved his body to the exact position I needed him to be in. "Get ready to observe the master."

Carolyn stepped forward and stood in the place she always stood when I asked her to marry me. Her eyes lit up and her smile widened. She was perhaps most alive in moments like this, as if this was as close as she was willing to come to destiny. And yet in that particular time, unbeknownst to them both, she was about to be pushed off the edge of the cliff.

"Carolyn, I want to you close your eyes."

"What do you mean?" she asked. "You've never asked me to do that before."

"Yes, but everything is different," I said. "Just trust me, okay?"

Carolyn closed her eyes and took a deep breath. I then looked over at Colin as if to say, "Be ready, my friend, your wish is about to come true." Then I began. It was the most heartfelt proposal of my life, for at that moment it seemed it would be the last time I would ever say such words. I was going to say everything I wanted to say to her, and though she would believe it was all an act, like the play we had enacted for years, only I would know the difference. I would not have any regrets this time for there would be nothing I left hidden, no gift that sat unopened at the side of our beloved tree.

Do you remember that moment, Great One? Does your memory extend back to that fateful moment when my life changed forever? How can birth and death come so close together, held apart by a single thread? Something died in me that night, but something new and fresh was born as well. Would I do it all again, knowing everything that would happen, all the things we lost and gained? Yes, I wouldn't change a thing, for it was the truest moment of my life, though I was about to lose the two people who meant more to me than anything else. I would step forward with the same confidence I had then without the slightest hesitation. It's wrong to try to change the moments that define us. Who knows what we'll be left with?

"Carolyn, your eyes are closed now because I cannot bear for you to look upon me when I say these words. My heart is so open that the slightest glance in the wrong direction might wound me in a way I cannot explain. If you were to turn your head away for even an instant I might run from you and never say the words that have cut through me these long years. You are both my salvation and my sword, destined to either save my life or slay me.

"You see, there is a place deep within me that has waited to hear a certain sound, a particular tone that has the power to transform my shattered existence. I have searched the whole world for that sound, hoping that one day it would drift past my ear and be caught in the net of my awareness, then sink into my soul where it would resonate with the vibrating strings of my heart. And what would I feel that fateful moment when grace descends upon me? It is easy to say now, for I recognized that music the moment I heard your voice. A song began that I longed to hear from the moment of my birth, and it continues as I stand here before you ready to say the words that may save us both.

"My dearest sweet Carolyn, this is the hour I have waited for, to see you standing before me and have the courage to bare my soul. Where does this courage come from? I have searched for it, longed to find the place where it hides, but it has eluded me like a mist and has cast shadows upon the life I have wanted to live. But every shadow must fade, and so now does this one end. I will throw aside every blanket that has hidden my desire and dissolve the boundaries that have kept me from your embrace. I stand now as a pilgrim who has traveled his whole life but to stand before this shrine and declare his undying love.

"And so, blinded as you are to the world of bodies and form, I ask that you go to that place where every secret is revealed and every heart is open. Rest for a moment in these words, Beloved Carolyn, for they are the truest words I will ever say to anyone."

Then I completed what I had set before me by grabbing hold of Colin's arm and moving him to the place where I just stood. He was startled but I held him tight so he couldn't move. Then I looked back at Carolyn and said the words that sealed our three fates forever.

"And now, I ask but one thing. Now that we have heard this sound, the melody that has awakened our lives, give to me the thing I most desire, for to taste this cup would fulfill me in a way no man can describe. Carolyn, as you open your eyes I ask that you give yourself to me now and always. Be my wife, Beloved, and my soul will rejoice."

Then Carolyn opened her eyes and saw Colin standing before her. It was as if she knew all along what was happening, as if she were prepared for the sight she beheld. Their eyes met and everything disappeared. Even I was gone, the man who had just opened his heart to reveal the life that kept him alive.

Then Colin said the only words he needed to say. "Will you?"

And Carolyn's heart filled with the love she had tried to disguise. "Yes, Colin, I will."

They fell into one another as if Heaven had fallen like rain into their arms. Nothing could stop the sudden flow of Divine Grace that lifted us above the clouds that night. Everything was complete, exactly as it was meant to be, and I reveled in the glory of our sacred accomplishment. Colin and Carolyn held each other with the passion I longed to give her, and I was overjoyed. It was also time for me to leave, to allow them their moment of grace.

Here's what you did not know. I walked away from you, Great Tree, drove back to my apartment, and packed my things. By morning I was in my car leaving L.A., and as I headed east on Interstate 10, I looked back for a final prayer.

"Enjoy every moment of love you have," I said to my friends, as if they could hear me. "Don't let a single day pass without opening the gift I've given you."

Chapter Three

By the mid-1980s, the hot subject everyone seemed obsessed with was soul mates. It became the modern Holy Grail, the great quest of everyone who was on a spiritual path. Many people who were married decided it was time to leave their current spouses to find their "real" partner, the person they had made a "soul-contract" with before they were born. If they weren't married already then it was the only thing on their minds, to find the perfect mate, the one who would stand beside them every step of the way, helping them move past the fearful patterns that had limited their lives. Fashions come and go, but the trend toward everything mystical was just gaining momentum. We had suddenly entered a "new age."

I should like to say that I was immune to this sort of nonsense, and that I had retained most of the cynical patterns that in the past allowed me to resist the tide of such fads. After all, I was by then a highly regarded novelist and was expected to set a good example. I wasn't supposed to follow trends, but to set them. At least that's what many of my friends in the literary field told me. After eighteen years in New York, one would think I had garnered a little good sense, the reasonable perspective my comrades seemed to have fashioned. But alas, I found myself falling into this esoteric trap and began reading as much as I could about soul mates, spiritual healing, astral travel, and a long list of other interests. The part of me that had once looked upon these subjects and the weak-minded people that followed them with contempt was not completely abandoned, but it was certainly taking a short nap.

Now and then I would call Carolyn and Colin and we would laugh about my sudden transformation. Carolyn was especially surprised because she had known me so long. Living in L.A., it was easy for her to follow each new passion that came bounding around the corner. But most New Yorkers considered themselves above such dependencies, preferring instead more traditional pursuits like the opera and designer drug abuse. Put those two things together and you have a perfect night in Manhattan. Things had changed, and I suddenly found myself standing in a place that was altogether unfamiliar, but satisfying nonetheless.

One night as I talked with Carolyn, I wondered how long it had been since I had seen my friends. It had not been since I married Florencia, I recalled, five years earlier. It was through Florencia that my transformation began, and I am eternally in her debt. The day we were married was the finest day of my life, but not without its own discomforts. Colin stood at my side when I took her hand, and in the corner of my eye I could see Carolyn, tears running down her cheeks. Why was she crying, I wondered? Did she feel the same mixture of joy and sadness I felt that moment? My best male friend was standing just to my right, the chosen witness to the event, the man I had turned the woman of my dreams over to many years before. It was the right move—I was sure of that. Carolyn and Colin seemed to have a wonderful marriage, and that's why I usually let so much time pass between visits. It was too hard to see them like that and not project my own face onto his, wishing it was me that was holding her, or that I had never turned her over to his arms. But Florencia changed everything.

I met her during a trip to Argentina seven years earlier, and for the first time since that fateful night when I left my friends in L.A., I felt my heart come alive. She was one of the most beautiful women I had ever met, and the contrast between her spirit and most of the other women I dated while living in New York was profound. I extended my visit just to stay with her, and the iceberg began to melt. I wasn't sure what was happening at the time, only that I could think of nothing but Florencia, which meant forgetting, at least for the moment, another woman I had been holding a sacred vigil for. Carolyn became a mist in the back of my mind, and until the moment I stood there on the altar watching her out of the corner of my eye, I had nearly forgotten the love I once felt.

Florencia came into my life like a cool wind over the hot desert. It took years for me to really believe she was mine, such was the wonder she inspired. I wrote several books where she played the heroine, the woman whose love was enough to rescue the man from certain demise. I changed her face and her name each time, but behind the words and plot there was always Florencia. "The whole world sings Florencia," was how I signed each letter I wrote to her, and I meant those words. She was my savior, my life, and the drink that kept me alive.

It was Florencia that changed everything for me, not Carolyn. Until then I lived like an oversexed monk, sleeping with every woman I could seduce while at the same time rejecting the outside world. The image of Carolyn's face haunted me for years after I left L.A., and it wasn't until I met the woman I was destined to marry that the flood began to recede. Her love was enough to lift me above the decaying shell of my life and awaken a place that had been sleeping within me for a very long time.

I was vacationing in Buenos Aires in 1978, escaping from the cold New York winter and the constant pressures of timetables and deadlines, when I met her. She was sitting alone in the lobby of the hotel where I was staying and I couldn't help walking over and starting a conversation. She was there to meet someone, a man who had obviously done me the great favor of not showing up. He didn't seem to mean that much to her, since she wasn't the least bit upset. I invited her to join me for dinner that night and she accepted.

Within minutes I realized that Florencia wasn't going to be one of my conquests. Looking back now, the constant flow of women through my life was my way of not letting go of Carolyn. Part of me felt that I had to be faithful to her, as insane as that now sounds, and I was being faithful as long as I reserved a place in my heart where no one else could enter. But the moment I met Florencia all that changed. I wanted her to come inside, to pry open the steel cage that held my heart hostage. After only a few hours I knew that I wanted her, I knew that she was the only woman that could break the spell cast by the woman I knew I loved but whom I could never have.

A year later she was living with me in New York and was able to get a good job as a private speech therapist. I proposed marriage while visiting her in Argentina earlier that summer, something that was harder than I first expected. I wanted to marry Florencia with my whole heart. But the idea of saying the words, the same sentiments I had expressed so many times before as a charade, brought back memories I didn't want to face. Somewhere in the back of my mind I had decided that I would never propose to another woman, and that I would never again set foot here beneath your branches, Great Tree. I didn't want to open that door, to grieve in the way I knew I needed if I was ever going to fully heal.

Another part of me knew that I had to move forward, to confront that demon and banish it from my mind once and for all. Florencia said I was her soul mate, and it was time for me to agree. She was the one who opened my eyes to the mystical life I now love, and I wanted to open my heart to her without reserve. But the proposal, yes, that was the most difficult for me. Would I be able to speak those magic words to her as I had to Carolyn? And if I did, would I be able to keep Carolyn's face at bay and focus on the woman I wanted to give my life to, the woman who wanted to hold me in her arms till she died?

There was a garden at Florencia's home in Argentina that we both loved. The flowers seemed to be in bloom every time I was there, more a testament of our love than of the garden itself. We would sit there for hours at a time and I would tell her all the things I held inside my heart during those forgotten years. I told her about the way I locked my heart away from the world, about the dreams I once held for love . . . but I never spoke to her about Carolyn. She didn't deserve such a weight, and I loved them both too much to compare. Florencia was the woman I wanted to marry, once and for all. For the first time in my life the woman I wanted, wanted me as well, and what joy that realization brought.

"Dearest Florencia," I said to her as we sat in that garden. "There are so many things I could say to you, so many poems I could write and sentiments I could share. And yet I find myself suddenly mute, as if it would be wrong for me to speak so openly. The love I feel for you can never be expressed in words, but in the feelings that lie behind the words . . . and this is what I most want to give you, Dearest. My heart opens and closes just as does my mouth, but no words stream from this rapid pulse. Only the love I feel for you, and the hope I am filled with whenever I am at your side.

"You know what I have come here to ask, and I will not waste another moment. Marry me, Florencia . . . say you'll be mine now and forever. Then I will do more than sing, but will live and breathe the song you give, and the melody will enliven my world in a way I cannot explain. Marry me, Florencia, and I will never stop singing."

It is impossible for me to describe what I felt the moment Florencia said yes. I had heard the word so many times before, every time I opened my heart to Carolyn hoping she would understand. But she never did. She just said the word as if I was someone else, the man she was really waiting for, Colin. How I loved them both, and I was glad it worked out the way it did. If it had been any other man I would have crawled inside my skin and never returned to the world of light. But my love for Colin was as strong as my love for her, and I realized how blessed the three of us were to have found one another.

But when Florencia said yes, I knew she meant it, not for someone else but for me. She wasn't dreaming of another man she had yet to meet; it was me she loved, and the love I felt for her that moment completely overwhelmed me. I broke down in her arms and wept, and she held me exactly the way I needed her to. "This is what it feels like," I thought to myself. "This is what it means to love a woman and have her love me back." Why did I run from this feeling for so long? I was nearly 55 years old and had finally found the love I had been waiting for.

Florencia was from a devoutly religious family, but in the years before we met she began to open to whole new areas of spirituality. At first I approached her schoolgirl enthusiasm with skepticism . . . and yet I wasn't about to make it a real issue. She meant too much to me by then. But the more she shared the more interested I became, and before long she was dragging me along to lectures at the Open Center in New York.

One day I heard a man named Ram Das speak, and it changed my life forever. He had been a professor at Harvard many years before but was fired because of his experiments with LSD, as Timothy Leary had been. He went to India, changed his name, and discovered a whole new level of mind expansion. I found myself considering ideas I never cared about before then. Other lectures followed and before I knew it I was hooked. Florencia was overjoyed.

"Do you know that I am your soul mate?" she asked me one day. "I knew it the moment we met. That is why I wasn't upset about being stood up. I felt something, and I knew you were for me."

"You know, I remember talking about this many years ago," I said to her. "Carolyn and I were discussing the same subject and I said that I had a feeling that there may be entire groups of people we come to earth to find."

"Yes, they call this, soul groups. Many people believe that we have a certain job to do on earth and we need to find the right people to help us. Sometimes we've been with those people for many lifetimes and we become so attached that we agree to return together again and again. And yet you are the only person I have ever felt this with. I don't know if I belong to a soul group or not."

I didn't want to tell her about the connection I had with Carolyn and Colin. She knew that we were all good friends, and she had of course met them at the wedding, but I felt uneasy divulging the full impact they had on my life. I knew exactly what Florencia meant, for I felt the same as she that first day together. But with Carolyn and Colin it was different. While Florencia was like a welcomed island where my love could rest and grow, there was work to be done with the others, and I wondered if I would ever find out what it was.

I was completely unprepared for the storm that lay ahead. My relationship with Florencia was about to be tested in a way none of us expected, the most dreadful manner possible. If there had only been a way for me to see the approaching earthquake before the ground began to shake beneath our feet, then perhaps I could have done something to slow its course. Maybe it would have swerved and chosen a different path, different lives to rip apart.

One morning as I was out for my daily walk I stopped at the corner newsstand to pick up the *Times*, just as I had done every morning for years. I nearly didn't see the article, the terrible news that shook my life. At first I thought it was a dream, as if some latent subconscious urge was working its way to the surface of my sleeping mind. But then I was horrified to realize that I wasn't dreaming and the photograph I was looking at was real.

British pop star Colin Church was killed in a tragic car accident yesterday near his Santa Monica home. Witnesses said that another car driven by an unidentified woman slammed into Church's vehicle at a traffic light, pinning it against a pole. Attempts to rescue the singer were hampered by the fact that he was pinned inside the car, and he was pronounced dead at the scene.

I cannot tell you, Great Tree, what happened after that. I may have blacked out altogether and roamed the streets in a daze. All I do know is that an hour later I was home, and Florencia was holding me in her arms. I stared at the wall and seemed unable to feel any emotions at all. All I knew was that he was gone, my dearest friend, my soul partner. But there was another.

The thought of Carolyn entered my mind. There was no mention of any other victims in the crash, no word at all of Colin's wife. Why didn't she call the moment she heard, I wondered as I dialed? Maybe she was in shock and was unable to think. I ran through every conceivable situation in my head as the phone rang and rang. Then finally, as I was ready to hang up, she answered.

"Hello." Her voice was broken and hoarse, and I knew immediately what was happening, how she felt, the devastation she was experiencing.

"Carolyn, it's me." That was all I needed to say to her. She knew what I was thinking and how I felt. I was probably the only person in the world who really knew what she was feeling.

"Get here," she cried. "For God's sake, get here."

I will always remember how Florencia helped me through those first few moments. She knew that I had to go alone, and that it had nothing to do with our relationship. I didn't even have to say a word to her about it. I was packing my bag and she was calling the airline. She drove me to JFK and held my hand the whole way. I couldn't help but think how lucky I was, and how unlucky. It hurt too much to think about her, about him . . . and what it all might mean.

A limo met me at LAX and drove me to Carolyn's house. I had never even seen the Santa Monica mansion Colin bought for her, but I had heard it was beautiful. As we pulled in through the gate I could see three other cars in the driveway, and I unconsciously began to hold my breath. We tried to stay out of each other's way for years, as if it made it easier to live our lives on two different coasts. But now we were the closest thing to family either one of us had. If we were going to descend into the dark cave of despair then we would do it together.

I could feel the grief beginning to well up inside me as the limo stopped and I got out. I walked toward the door and hesitated before touching the doorbell. An older Hispanic woman answered, the maid I think, and she stepped aside to let me in.

"You are Mr. James, yes?" she asked.

"Yes, I am. Is Carolyn . . ."

"She is in the bedroom upstairs. No one else can come she said . . . only you."

I walked up the long staircase that led to the bedrooms as if I had lead feet. In the living room downstairs I could hear voices I did not recognize, friends that were gathered to mourn the death of their friend.

"It's probably Fredrick James, the writer." One of them said. "They were all very close you know."

"Yes, Colin was his best man a few years ago. Wow. What a blow."

The tears were starting to well up in my eyes, and seconds later I saw one of the upstairs doors open and Carolyn stepped out.

"Fredrick, thank God you're here," she said as she ran toward me. I ran too and threw my arms around her. Our bodies shook as we held each other, as if we had been waiting till I arrived to really fall apart. For a moment it felt as if we were one person, and our tears fell like the beating of a drum upon the floor. The suede jacket I wore muffled the sound of her crying, and I felt my own eyes swell shut, as if I was finally beginning to feel. We had lost one of the most important people in both our lives, and now we were alone, exactly the way we started.

I hardly left her side during those next few days. The constant flow of people to the house, not to mention the reporters and mourning fans who kept a vigil outside, seemed to exhaust Carolyn. She held her head up high when she was in public, but when we were alone together her real feelings rushed out like a flood of water. I sat with her in her room, in their room, and often wondered what it was like when Colin was there. I held Carolyn in my arms while she wept over the loss of her husband, and I felt the loss of a member of my own soul family. No one outside that door understood what we felt. The void we experienced in our grief and loss seemed insurmountable.

The funeral was exceptionally well planned and was attended by many celebrities, all the people Colin had worked with or influenced over the years. Once again Carolyn held strong and said all the right words to all the right people. She was splendid, and everyone was impressed by the way she seemed to be pulling herself together. Only I knew what lay beneath the surface, the river of fear that was rushing underneath the well-practiced smile. She waited till we were alone then expressed with her eyes all the things she could never say to the others, about how alone she suddenly felt, how much she missed Colin, and how afraid she was. And I would reach out for her hand and we stood there looking at each other, thankful that someone else understood.

I talked to Florencia every day while I was away in California. Her voice grounded me and made me feel like everything was going to return to normal someday. But there was something else I felt, something I could never tell her. There was a strange distance between us, like the seam of a shirt that was beginning to wear and split apart. I didn't know if she noticed it or not, but it was building inside me. Maybe it was just the stress, or maybe it was something more. I couldn't even think about that at the time, for to add Florencia to the equation was too much for me. I tried to convince myself that it was just a fantasy, a knee-jerk reaction to the loss of my friend.

I decided to stay in L.A. for several weeks to help Carolyn readjust. Colin had been her whole world. She was no longer active in the art community and never spent much time away from the house. They seemed to have had the perfect relationship, just as I knew they would, which made the loss even more profound.

After two weeks I started to catch glimpses of the Carolyn I missed so much. It was always while we were doing simple things, like shopping for produce. She would look at me and a smile that I hadn't seen in years would erupt across her face. It hadn't been since we stood here beneath your branches years earlier that we looked at one another like that. I had been so careful to hide my feelings since that night, to suppress the overpowering passion I felt for Carolyn. I helped them break free into the marriage that fed them all those years and I wasn't about to cripple it with my own attachment.

When did it all begin to change, Great Tree? Maybe she had to face being alone, and it scared her in a way she could not explain. Or maybe there was something more, a spark she recognized that she was finally mature enough to acknowledge. To me it felt like a warm breeze that caressed and soothed me, bringing with it the promise of spring. But what would I do with all those smiles that told me more than I was ready to hear. I wasn't prepared for such a shift, even if I had waited my whole life to feel such grace. For the first time since I knew Carolyn I was afraid, not of losing her but of having my dream come true.

Carolyn was studying me. I don't know how else to explain it, but it felt as if she was looking at me for the first time, looking past the friendship that had nurtured us toward something deeper, a possibility she had never seen before. Why did I want to run from her, Great Tree? These are the questions that haunt me now as I look back over the years. I began to see signs of my own longing reflected in her eyes. It is a strange thing to have your dreams come true, especially when you're no longer capable of embracing them.

As the weeks wore on I could feel us returning to a familiar rhythm. So many years had passed since we walked those streets together, laughed with such abandon, and cried with such intensity. I could feel Colin's presence in it all, as if he were watching us, encouraging us to move forward. I imagined that he wanted us to be together, for it was the only way we could keep him alive. If it were only so simple, I thought to myself. Even if Carolyn was opening to me in a new way, which was still conjecture on my part, what was I prepared to do about it? Was I willing to forsake my life with Florencia and embrace a cloud I had been chasing most of my life? I was no longer thirty years old, and life was not as simple as it was then. I could feel the most important moment of my life approaching, and I had no idea how I would react when it arrived.

My calls to Florencia increased, and I think she sensed my confusion. I could feel myself grasping for straws, though no real romantic alternative had even presented itself with Carolyn. Maybe I was reading more into her cues than really existed. Maybe it was my own hidden desire to fulfill the most profound call of my life, to love her and empty my soul into her heart. I began to actually hope that it was the case, that I had misread the whole scene. Then I could kiss Carolyn and leave when it was time, then return to my wife. I would get on the jet and smile as I walked down the runway, then call her when I arrived in New York. She would thank me for seeing her through the hardest period of her life and I would tell her that that's what best friends are for. Then I would make love to Florencia and fall into her the way I wanted to, and all the world would be right again.

But there was one thought that haunted my mind: What did Colin want?

The day before I was scheduled to leave for New York was perhaps the hardest day of my life. Though we were normally very affectionate, to the point that the average passerby would assume that we were already married, on that particular day Carolyn didn't seem to want to let go. She held onto me as if I was her life raft, as if my leaving meant she would finally be alone, which was her greatest fear. She had lost Colin and now she was going to lose me again. I could feel her becoming more and more attached, and it was only natural for her to search for a way to keep me there. I could tell by the way she was looking at me what was going to happen next, and I had no idea how I would respond.

We had dinner at our favorite Italian restaurant that night, a little out-of-the-way place in Hollywood, then headed back to Santa Monica. Neither one of us said a word in the car, as if we were afraid of what we would say given the chance. But I could feel what was in Carolyn's heart as she caressed my hand, almost as if she was pulling me back to you, Great Tree.

"Turn here," she said.

We took a right on Windsor and slowly drove past the houses that still separated us from you. I didn't say a word, for if I did I would have revealed more than I wanted to reveal. It was the moment I had been waiting for, and the moment I dreaded most. We pulled in front of the yard and got out of the car.

"Come on," she said as she took my hand. "We need to pay our respects."

I hadn't seen you in so many years, Great One, and you hadn't changed at all. Your green branches hung like a canopy over our heads and greeted us with open arms, the same way you always greeted us through those long years. I had forgotten how it felt to stand here, to look up at the moon through the leaves and feel the cool wind as it blew between us. Memories began to flood into my mind, all those proposals I said and meant, and the way Carolyn looked past them all. I remembered the day Colin and Carolyn finally expressed their love, and I could see myself walk away as they held one another for the first time. Then I looked over and saw Carolyn again, an older Carolyn, but just as beautiful as she was the day I first met her. She was smiling at me, the kind of smile that says more than words ever can.

"I have a favor to ask of you," she finally said. "I've been thinking about all the nights we stood here beneath this tree, all the words that were said, and all the things that were left unsaid. So many years have passed . . . I can see things now that I didn't see then. I think I have a sense for what was really going on, what you were feeling. I'm a bit ashamed, really. How could I have been so blind, so stupid?"

I reached out and took her hand. "Everything worked out the way it was meant to, Carolyn."

"Yes, it did. I had eighteen wonderful years with Colin . . . the best years of my life. But I'm also just now beginning to see something else, something that was right in front of me the whole time."

"And what was that?" I asked.

"It was you. You and I have talked about soul mates over the years, and now I realize that that's what we are. Certainly Colin was part of that, but it began here, beneath this tree, you telling me how much you loved me and me being too blind to understand."

"Like I said—"

"No, let me finish. This is something I should have said to you a long time ago. I just didn't know how . . . I was too afraid. And now, as we stand here again, there's something I need to do. You taught me so much, Fredrick, and now everything has changed. Now it's my turn."

"What do you mean?"

"You've always been the one to propose here . . . and now I need you to listen. I want to reverse the roles, just this one time. Let me say to you the words that can set us both free. Give me the favor of looking into your eyes and asking you to be mine forever."

I was swimming in an ocean of light, and I didn't know what to say to her. My dream was being realized at last . . . the words of love I had tied to each one of your branches were about to fall upon my own ears, to be absorbed by my own heart. Was it real, or was it the same dramatization that had always taken place in your shadow? And what would I say if it was real? I had no answer for these questions, only the nodding of my head that told Carolyn to begin.

"Fredrick, I have loved you my whole life without realizing it. You are the very constancy that has defined my existence, the heart that has been hidden from my sight but which has never once stopped beating for me. If I could go back to those early days and hear you express your love to me again, then I would do so in an instant. The words still echo in my mind, as if they were recorded there and will never disappear. Whenever

I'm lonely I listen to them again, and I think of the way you looked into my eyes when you proposed. How could I have not recognized that light, the spark of your heart that reached out to enfold me?

"I am not here to ask for your forgiveness, but to fulfill both our longing. The mantle has now fallen to me, my dearest Fredrick, and so it is my voice that will pull the angel's song into this earthly realm in hope that it will reverberate within us both. I ask but one gift, one final favor that will illumine my dark night. Say you will be mine. Say you will marry me, Fredrick, and stand at my side for all time. It is the only thing I want now, the only thing that can satisfy me. Give this gift to me and I will rejoice for finding the love I have denied till now."

I could hardly contain my heart. Her words filled the empty void in a way I did not expect. Carolyn loved me, and you witnessed her words. For an instant I felt that I was thirty again and that our lives were in front of us. We would be married and my dream would be realized. I looked into her eyes, just as she had looked into mine each time I had proposed. I knew then that there was only one thing I could say to her, the only real gift I could give.

"Yes, Carolyn, I will marry you. I am yours forever."

She smiled at me, but she knew what was happening. It was a play, just as it had always been. She knew that I would be on my way back to New York in the morning and would rejoin my wife. Nothing was going to change in the real world, for we had come too far to go back. I would never leave Florencia, no matter how much I loved Carolyn. You were but the stage where we declared our love, Great Tree, the place where we said words that we would never say otherwise. I took her hand as if to tell her all this, and she understood.

"It feels good," she said to me as a single tear fell from her eye. "Now I know how you felt all those years."

Chapter Four

Two things happened in 1999 that changed my life. Florencia died in March after a short bout with breast cancer. Happily, our lives were filled with joy when she left and I'm glad she didn't suffer much. By the time we realized what was happening the cancer had advanced to the stage where there was nothing we could do. We spent those last weeks together laughing and crying, but mostly holding each other and being very quiet. I turned seventy a week after she passed, and I swear I could feel her looking down upon me.

Something else happened that year that I will describe to you now, Great Tree. It began a month after my wife's death when I decided to leave New

York. I could no longer bear to look out over that city and see the woman I missed everywhere I turned. There were benches in Central Park where we used to sit for hours looking out over the fields with children playing and lovers sitting together in the grass. And how many restaurants had her name written there, the special hideaways I loved to bring her to, the places no one else seemed to know about but us. Everywhere I looked I saw Florencia's smile, and it ripped my heart apart.

I longed for warmer weather, for a city I knew and understood, a place where I could begin my life again, or renew a very ancient life I never had the chance to live. I decided to return to Los Angeles. I had a friend there, the kind of friend most people are never lucky enough to have, someone who would welcome me home with a full heart and open arms. That friend was Carolyn, and I wondered if we too would turn like the seasons toward a vibrant new life.

We kept in close contact since Colin's death, our way of maintaining the connection the three of us always shared. Carolyn came to visit us in New York often and developed a strong friendship with Florencia. We never talked about the last time we stood here beneath your branches, Proposing Tree, as if denying that moment would help us move forward. I thought about it often though, about the love she expressed to me, words I had longed to hear for so many years. I knew I made the right decision, but it haunted me, as if I had thrown away the love I had spent my whole life searching for. She had come to New York for Florencia's funeral and I was glad she was there. She held my hand just as I held hers when we lost Colin. I wanted to pull her in even closer, but the snow was piled so deep around my heart, paralyzing me, and spring felt so far away.

But the months passed and spring did arrive. The city was alive with new possibilites, and it was time for me to step away from the past and accept the change. A new life was on the horizon, and yet it felt like a return to a distant past.

What would happen now, I wondered? Would the tumblers of our lives finally fall into place enabling us to take the step we never had the courage to entertain before? Carolyn had not remarried after Colin's death. A few men entered then left her life, but none of them could hold a candle to the one she gave everything to. She lived with a memory, while another part of her mind wondered what the future might hold. Could there ever be another man who would understand the passion she held in her heart? I hoped that man was me, that the love she expressed so many years earlier was still alive, like a candle in front of a shrine that burns for many nights waiting for the Beloved to come and recognize its light.

I didn't tell Carolyn I was coming. I knew she would feel the heaviness of my approach just as I was feeling it, and it was a bittersweet weight. It had been forty years since we met in that L.A. restaurant and so much had transpired since then, bringing us close then forcing us apart. Was it possible for two people who had changed so much to remember what it felt like to be young, and love each other in a way that seems impossible for most? I could feel the twilight of my own days bearing down upon me, and there was only one thing I wanted to realize before I left the world altogether.

I checked into a hotel two blocks from Carolyn's home. She had long since sold the house in Santa Monica and bought a condo, just a short walk from you, the tree where I am sitting now. Why did she return? How many promises still lie beneath these branches even when my life seems near its end? There was still one final scene for us to perform, one final proposal for me to recite here at your base, great tree.

As I unpacked my suitcase and sat down on the bed, I wondered if it would finally become real.

I knew my friend so well, and that is why I knew she would come. We had wrapped so many dreams around these branches, and they fell to the earth like seeds that grow in a later season. Carolyn loved to take long walks through the neighborhood at night, especially when the air was cool and the moon was full. It was early September and a gentle wind blew through your leaves, and it made completing this long journey feel like a dream. No one was living in the house at the time, and so I didn't think anyone would mind if I hired a crew to string the tiny white Christmas lights through your branches. People stopped and wondered, but no one pressed the question. It took several hours to get it right, to make it look as it had so many years earlier when Carolyn and I stood here and pronounced the words that would shape both our lives, the last time the three of us were here together. By six o'clock they were finished, and so I sat down to watch and wait.

I will never forget what it felt like sitting there, waiting for her. My mind was like a movie screen and my memory cast images upon that white surface that I thought I had forgotten. I remembered how we looked as a young man and woman sitting here, then years later when she held my hand and tried to claim my heart. It was as if I was reliving every moment, and I could feel my heart expand and contract with each breath I breathed. My whole life seemed to exist in your shadow, great tree, or at least the life I clung to in my mind. Nothing came close to those feelings and dreams, even the many happy years I spent with my beloved Florencia. I held my hand against your bark and felt happy for the first time in months. Waiting for Carolyn was my life's calling, and I would not end this vigil till it was complete.

I did not need to see her silhouette to know she was coming. The energy seemed to rise from the earth and fill my body, as if you too were anxious to witness this final scene. Then I looked down the street and saw her slender form on the sidewalk, and I knew the moment had come at last. She was walking at a fast pace, but then seemed to slow down when she came close to you. And I knew what she was thinking. "Why are the lights out so early? No one decorates their tree, especially this tree, so early." I was sitting on the far side of the trunk where she could not see me, and I watched as she stepped onto the grass twenty feet away.

"Who put those lights on you?" she asked out loud, as if you had ears to hear her.

I stood up and positioned my body where she could see me. At first she seemed confused, as if none of it made sense at all. Then she understood what was happening, and stepped toward me.

"What do you think?" I asked her. "Sort of reminds me . . ."

"Yes, I know . . . I should have known right away."

By then she was so close I could feel the warmth of her skin upon my own. I reached out and touched her face, and she took hold of my hand and held it firm against her cheek.

"Why are you here, old man?"

I didn't answer her, not with words anyway, and she suddenly knew why I came. We stood there looking at each other for a very long time, yet neither one of us spoke a word. We both knew what it meant, where it would lead, and how our lives would suddenly change. It was the first time we stood here beneath your branches and didn't propose to one another. For the first time in our lives we didn't need to.

The woman closed the manuscript and looked up at the tree. "Is it possible?" she asked. "Could all this really have happened right here in my own yard, beneath this very tree?" Then she stood up suddenly as if an electric current shot through her body. "But how does it end? He never wrote what happened. I can't be left hanging like this. I have to know if she said . . . if he said . . . if they're together now."

She walked over to the Proposing Tree and looked up through the ancient branches. Then she closed her eyes and tried to imagine how Fredrick and Carolyn must have felt standing there. Then she tried to imagine the day they brought Colin, and the final day when words weren't needed at all. So many passionate moments, she thought to herself. So many dreams that fell like leaves onto the ground. And she was lucky enough to hear the story, the story that no human was meant to hear, only the Tree.

"Mom, when are you going to come inside?" It was her son calling to her, and she realized how lost she had been in the story. It was time to return to the ordinary world where men and women have families and attend to everyday responsibilities. For a moment she wanted to sit beneath the tree, the Proposing Tree, and dream of Carolyn and Fredrick, wondering what might have happened to them, or even fill in the blanks with her own fantasy ending. But the

intoxication of such a moment might make her never want to return to her life again, and her son needed her.

"I'll be there in a moment, Honey. I just had to finish reading that manuscript you found."

She looked up at the clouds that rolled by, then walked up the steps to the front door. The book was held tight in her hand. She couldn't seem to let it go just then.

Weeks passed, and the woman found herself sitting in her familiar chair more than she had before, staring at the tree as if it had more mysteries to tell. Her son played nearby, and she never lost sight of him. All the while she dreamed of romance, of the love that had been lit like a fire a few feet from where she sat. She longed for romance in her own life, even if she wasn't able to admit to such a disquieting thought. She had been married for eleven years, and there was really nothing for her to complain about. Her husband was a fabulous provider, and though no one ever accused him of being overly affectionate, he had his own way of showing he cared. He did work more than she hoped, though, and there never seemed to be much time when he came home at night to rekindle the flame that had drawn them together when they were young. She wondered if their love would be strong enough to survive the same tests that Carolyn and Fredrick's had.

She closed her eyes and tried to remember the manuscript she had read, the book she was not meant to find that served as a door to another world. She tried to picture them in her mind, all the people who were more than characters she found in a story. They were real, she was sure of it, and she longed to know more. She hoped her dream would catapult her to the past, forty or so years before when Fredrick first proclaimed his heart. Then she could listen and feel the amazing rush of light that passed between them that day, and continued for decades.

When she opened her eyes again she was surprised to see an old man standing on the sidewalk looking at her as she sat. Then his eyes looked toward the tree, and he seemed to be lost in a world only he could see. Hesitantly, the young woman walked over to him and smiled.

"Hello," she said. "I don't mean to disturb you, but this is my house. We moved here a few months ago. Do you live here in the neighborhood?"

There was something about his eyes that soothed her soul, as if he understood love in a manner that words could never say. He smiled at her, then tipped his hat.

"It's nice to meet you. Yes, I do live nearby, right around the corner actually. I've been coming here, in one way or another I guess, for a very long time."

"It's a beautiful neighborhood," she continued. "And this tree . . . it's majestic and wonderful . . . don't you think?"

"This tree? Yes, I think you could say that. This is a very special tree. There's magic beneath these branches, you know."

She smiled, as if she didn't need to ask him anything else. "My name is Maggie. What is your name?"

"Fredrick . . . Fredrick James," he said as he held out his hand.

"Fredrick James . . . I think I've heard of you. You're a writer, aren't you? I think I read something you wrote."

"Now that would be a surprise," he laughed. "I haven't written anything for many years. You must have stolen one of your mother's books."

"Yes, maybe I did. Well, it's wonderful to meet you Mr. James."

"Please, call me Fredrick."

"Fredrick then." She bit her lip, wanting to ask one more question but not wanting to be too obvious. She had to know how the book ended, but she didn't want him to know about her son finding the manuscript. Was Carolyn still alive? Did they walk away from the tree that night arm in arm after forty years of being apart?

"I was wondering," she finally said, "are you married, Fredrick?"

He looked at her strangely, as if he didn't know what to say. Then he looked to his left and pointed down the street.

"Yes, I am," he said. "In fact, here comes my wife now."

A tall, slender woman with radiant eyes walked up and put her arm around Fredrick. They looked at one another with eyes that defied the years of separation, all those broken dreams and nights spent sitting and dreaming beneath the Proposing Tree. They were in love, a deep incomprehensible love that could never be described in a book or in a song. It was exactly as Maggie imagined them.

"This is Carolyn," Fredrick said to her. "Honey, this nice woman and her family moved into the house a little while back . . . and she admires the tree."

Carolyn's eyes lit up. "Oh, the tree. Well this is a very special tree. I could tell you stories about this tree you wouldn't believe."

"Oh, I think I might believe them. There's magic beneath those branches. I can feel it."

Seeds still fall from your branches, and in time they will sink into the ground to inspire new dreams. Others will come here and stand in your shadow, and their hearts will feel the rapid approach of a longing they may not understand with their minds, but which their hearts will fully embrace. Eyes will look into other eyes, and hearts into other hearts, and they will know why they came here, just as Carolyn and I know. We all come for love, for it is the only thing worthy of our visions. In the end, it is the one thing that really matters in this world.

We came walking past you last night, Great Tree, as we have done so many times before, and for the first time we felt as if you no longer belonged to us. You had already worked your magic on us, and now it was time for these others, the two who live beside you now. There was a look in the woman's eyes that I recognized, for I knew what visions lay in her heart; dreams of the man, her husband, being transformed as we were once transformed, giving his heart to her as he promised he would. Carolyn and I stopped, for we did not want to intrude upon their moment of grace. He reached for her hand and I knew what was happening. It was their tree now, and it was time for us to walk away and live the final years of our lives. The day would come when they would pass you on to others whose lives would be sheltered by your branches. But for now it was for them, for their hearts and for the love they once promised to each other. I leaned over and kissed Carolyn's lips, knowing a new chapter had begun.

"Love is an amazing virtue," I said to her.

"It's all we have and all we need," she answered.

Free CD Offer

Would you like to receive my newest CD as a special promotion? "For the Beloved" contains some of the most beautiful music I have ever written, and it is the perfect addition to the romance of *The Proposing Tree*. Many of the songs have been saved for this very special CD, and it is sure to open your heart.

Order by credit card on-line at

www.emissaryoflight.com/bestofcd/htm.

Or, send a check or money order for U.S. $6.00 (to cover shipping and handling costs) to:

Free CD
Beloved Community
48 Morse Ave.
Ashland, OR 97520

Be sure to include your name and address!

If you have problems with your order, please don't contact the publisher! Instead, e-mail us at: bestof@belovedcommunity.org.

Please allow up to four weeks for domestic delivery.

Hampton Roads Publishing Company

. . . for the evolving human spirit

Hampton Roads Publishing Company
publishes books on a variety of subjects,
including metaphysics, health,
visionary fiction, and other related topics.

For a copy of our latest catalog, call toll-free
800-766-8009, or send your name and address to:

Hampton Roads Publishing Company, Inc.
1125 Stoney Ridge Road
Charlottesville, VA 22902

e-mail: hrpc@hrpub.com
www.hrpub.com